Fun in the Sun

By Amy Ackelsberg
Illustrated by Laura Thomas

Grosset & Dunlap
An Imprint of Penguin Group (USA) Inc.

GROSSET & DUNLAP

Published by the Penguin Group

Penguin Group (USA) Inc., 375 Hudson Street, New York, New York 10014, USA

Penguin Group (Canada), 90 Eglinton Avenue East, Suite 700, Toronto, Ontario M4P 2Y3, Canada

(a division of Pearson Penguin Canada Inc.)

Penguin Books Ltd, 80 Strand, London WC2R 0RL, England

Penguin Ireland, 25 St Stephen's Green, Dublin 2, Ireland (a division of Penguin Books Ltd)

Penguin Group (Australia), 707 Collins Street, Melbourne, Victoria 3008, Australia

(a division of Pearson Australia Group Pty Ltd)

Penguin Books India Pvt Ltd, 11 Community Centre, Panchsheel Park, New Delhi—110 017, India

Penguin Group (NZ), 67 Apollo Drive, Rosedale, Auckland 0632, New Zealand (a division of Pearson New Zealand Ltd)

Penguin Books (South Africa), Rosebank Office Park, 181 Jan Smuts Avenue, Parktown North 2193, South Africa

Penguin China, B7 Jiaming Center, 27 East Third Ring Road North, Chaoyang District, Beijing 100020, China

Penguin Books Ltd., Registered Offices: 80 Strand, London WC2R 0RL, England

ISBN 978-0-448-46474-9   10 9 8 7 6 5 4 3 2 1

It was a beautiful summer day in Berry Bitty City. The sun was shining, butterflies were fluttering about in the breeze, and there wasn't a cloud in the sky.

"What perfect weather for a day at the beach with our berry best friends!" Strawberry Shortcake said to Plum Pudding as they loaded their scooters with beach gear.

Soon, all of Strawberry's friends had gathered for the trip.
"Are you ready for some fun in the sun?" asked Cherry Jam.
"Yes!" cried Raspberry Torte.

"I brought my pail and shovel," said Orange Blossom. "I want
to build a sand castle!"
"I can't wait to read my favorite books!" said Blueberry Muffin.
"Do you know the best thing about the beach?" asked Plum Pudding.

"The ocean!" cried Strawberry, Orange, and Blueberry.
"I love to jump in the waves!" exclaimed Cherry.

"I want to swim underwater!" said Raspberry.

"What about you, Lemon?" asked Plum. "What's your favorite thing about the ocean?"

"I'm not sure," said Lemon. She looked a little worried.

"Time to go!" interrupted Strawberry.

The girls hopped on their scooters and zoomed off.

Before long, Strawberry and her friends were bobbing up and down in the surf. Orange and Cherry were diving for shells. Strawberry and Plum were riding the waves. Raspberry and Blueberry were practicing their swim strokes.

Everyone was having a great time in the ocean. Everyone except . . .

"Lemon!" called Orange. "Don't you want to come in?"
Just then, a berry big wave crashed onto the shore.
"I don't think so," replied Lemon. She put her head down
and went back to reading her book.

"Hmm," said Plum. "I wonder why Lemon doesn't want to swim."
"Maybe she'll join us later," Blueberry replied.

After a while, the girls got out of the water.

"All that swimming has made me berry hungry!" said Orange as she handed out sandwiches and drinks.

"Yum!" said Cherry. "These fruit smoothies are so refreshing!"

When they were done eating, the girls relaxed and read their books.

Next, Cherry turned on some music, and her friends bopped to the beat.
"I love this song!" exclaimed Plum.

After that, the girls took turns burying one another in the sand.
"Do you like my seaweed necklace?" asked Strawberry.

Suddenly, Blueberry jumped up. "Last one in the water is a rotten berry!" she cried.

"Wait for us!" exclaimed Strawberry, Plum, Orange, Cherry, and Raspberry as they ran toward the waves.

Lemon was the only one who stayed behind.
"Are you coming, Lemon?" Raspberry asked.
"No," Lemon replied. "I . . . I think I ate too much—my stomach hurts!"

Lemon sat on the beach, while her friends laughed and splashed in the water.

"I wish Lemon were with us," Orange said. "She's missing all the fun!"
Strawberry looked at Lemon sitting by herself. She seemed berry sad.
"I'll go check on her," said Strawberry, heading toward the shore.

"Lemon, you haven't gone in the water all day," said Strawberry. "Is something wrong?"

"Oh, Strawberry, I'm not a berry good swimmer," Lemon confessed. "I'm scared to go in the ocean!"

"It's okay to be afraid!" Strawberry told Lemon. "The ocean is big, and we're berry bitty. That's why we all swim together—to look out for one another!"

Strawberry gave Lemon a hug as the rest of the girls joined them onshore.
"You don't have to go in the water if you don't want to," Orange told Lemon.
"But we're here for you if you change your mind!" added Raspberry.

Strawberry and her friends spent the rest of the day building a giant sand castle on the beach.

Before they packed up to go home, Lemon looked out at the ocean one last time.

"Hmm . . . ," she said. "Maybe I should give it a try."

"Are you sure?" asked Blueberry.

"Yes," said Lemon.

"Are you okay, Lemon?" asked Strawberry.
"I'm fine," Lemon replied. Then she gave her friends a big hug.
"The ocean isn't as scary as I thought," she said. "Especially when I have my berry best friends by my side!"